DANI BENNONI Long May He Live

DANI BENNONI

Long May He Live

Bart Moeyaert

TRANSLATED FROM THE FLEMISH BY

Wanda Boeke

FRONT STREET
Asheville, North Carolina

Also by Bart Moeyaert:

Bare Hands

Hornet's Nest

It's Love We Don't Understand

Brothers

First U.S. edition, 2008

LIBRARY OF CONGRESS CATALOGING-IN-PUBLICATION DATA
Moeyaert, Bart.
  Dani Bennoni / Bart Moeyaert ; translated from the Flemish by Wanda J.
Boeke. — 1st U.S. ed.
    p. cm.
    Summary: In the summer of 1939, with his brother serving in the military,
ten-year-old Bing asks his older neighbor, Dani, to repay a debt by teaching
him to play soccer, but Dani refuses and sets Bing and his friend Lenny on a
course for revenge.
  ISBN 978-1-932425-97-0 (hardcover : alk. paper)
  [1. Interpersonal relations—Fiction. 2. Revenge—Fiction. 3. Soccer—Fiction.
4. Belgium—History—1914—Fiction.] I. Boeke, Wanda. II. Title.
  PZ7.M7227Dan 2008
  [Fic]—dc22

                                    2007018578

FRONT STREET
An Imprint of Boyds Mills Press, Inc.
815 Church Street
Honesdale, Pennsylvania 18431

DANI BENNONI Long May He Live

ONE

I have Mone's shoes on. In the toes there are wads of paper. The rubber bands around my kneesocks stretch tight. They're cutting off my lower legs. My toes hurt, my feet are half asleep, but I don't let on. I walk straight across the soccer field.

Right into the center circle Lenny walks with me. He's still saying things to boost my courage long after I can't hear him anymore.

I keep walking. In the corner of the field stands Dani Bennoni. He is finished with his training session. He trains every day.

"Go, Bing, go!" cries Lenny far behind me, as if I were a whole team by myself.

I put the ball under my arm down, and place my foot on top of it.

"Dani Bennoni," I say. "I want to learn how to play soccer."

Dani looks at me. For a second he thinks I'm my brother in these clothes, but I'm not my brother. He can see that, two heads' difference. He looks at the ball I'm resting my foot on. He looks at my feet. He nods once. Who wouldn't recognize Mone's shoes?

"I mean it," I say. "I want to know how."

Dani stares at me and only after a while closes his mouth because his tongue is dry from being open to the air.

"Why?" he asks.

"Because," I say. "Did you forget about yesterday?"

A little sound comes out of Dani's throat.

"Oh, that," he says.

He points at my shorts. Just like my shoes, they don't fit. As if I didn't know that. I had to tie a knot in the waistband to keep them from falling down. I know a lot of material is bunched together above my knees, because of course Mone's jersey is also much too big for me, but I'm not going to start cutting. I won't do that. We're keeping everything the way it is.

"And that has to happen now?" asks Dani. He rubs his hand over his short hair. "Today?"

"Today," I say. "You don't have any more money. You'll have to say yes."

Dani quickly looks around. "You watch your mouth," he says.

I pluck a key out of the air and lock up my mouth. I throw the key away over my shoulder.

"Sure," I say. "I'll watch my mouth, and you keep your word."

I spread my arms and point at myself so that he can size me up from top to toe. Swimming, I've got an old pair of swimming trunks for that. Swimming I already know how to do. I'm talking about soccer. Can't Dani see the number 7 on my back? Doesn't he remember what Mone did in the Daring Club?

"Bing!" says Dani, and his voice shoots into the higher ranges. "Think it over, kid. I'm sure there's something else I can give you." He looks straight at me and lets his mouth open up and his face too, and suddenly a sound comes out of it that resembles laughter but doesn't sound nice. *Ha haa*, it booms, and the trees around the field join in.

My foot slips off the ball. I bend over to pick it up and tuck it under my arm, where it was at first, but the feeling's not the same. My head has gotten heavier, my arms shorter. I can't stand up as nice and straight anymore.

"You and a ball," says Bennoni. "You and a ball." He chuckles a little more and shakes his head. "You can't play soccer. You know that. You can tell by your arms and legs, and by your feet."

He lifts one of his legs and shakes his foot loosely. "Do it? Do it?"

I imitate him. I don't do it right. My hips shouldn't be shaking. My foot should be shaking. It's not doing it yet. Of course it's not doing it, I haven't learned anything yet.

"You'll never score like that," says Dani. He almost has to laugh again.

"You're going to teach me," I say. To show that I really want to learn, am even impatient to, I lift my legs in turn and try to shake my feet.

"Your foot," says Dani. "Your foot." He sighs. "I'd like to teach you, Bing, it's not that. Maybe it'll work, maybe by accident you'll even kick the ball. But from where I stand, it's a lost cause."

He quickly looks from me to his own shoes and back and gives me a smile.

"How old are you now, ten? I don't want to knock you, kid, but look: there are soccer players and there are—" He rubs his middle finger over his thumb and tries to find a word in the air. "There are—" Finally he lets his arms drop alongside his body and gives his shoulders a shrug. He gets no further than: "Other kids."

"Others," I say.

"Right," he says, and he pats my cheek. "Aren't you good with your hands?"

"Yup," I say, and I raise my hands.

"Well, then," says Dani. He grabs his Daring Club bag and leaps over the fence. "Just stick to your hands." He looks over his shoulder and winks at me. "Go draw. Go fiddle with something. Bye, Bing."

I give him a nod. "Bye, Dani," I say.

Behind me comes the sound of a sigh that's deeper than mine. Lenny has come over to me. He's panting. Lenny gets tired quickly.

"So, no go," he says.

"Yeah, no go," I say.

"Okay," says Lenny. "Then we'll do step two. Come on."

TWO

The door opens and Martha is standing in front of us.
I take hold of Mone's jersey between thumb and forefinger, as if it had the lapels of a jacket, bow deeply, and
say that she has been sent a hello.

"Who from?" asks Martha.

I quickly glance at Lenny. We agreed that we're not
going to lie. We'll just hold our tongues at the right
moment. That's different.

"Who *could* you get a hello from?" I ask with a little
chuckle.

Martha's face brightens. She takes a step forward,
pulls the door behind her until it's open just a crack,
and slaps her hands in front of her large mouth.

"You're kidding. Really?" she asks. She glances
from me to Lenny to make sure we're thinking of the
same name she is.

"Of course really," I say, and I thump myself on the

chest, because until now I haven't lied. I haven't said who sent the hello. No name dropped from my lips. That's how I arranged it with Lenny. We're going to try without lies to get to where we have to be today: out on the field with Dani.

As a distraction, I start singing—that Johnny Hess song, *Je Suis Swing*. Everybody's singing it. Martha is supposed to think that the song goes along with the hello.

She thinks we're a gift, especially me. That's how she looks. She beams and she blushes. Her lips form a name—straightaway the one we want: Dani Bennoni.

Martha's mother calls from inside the house, wants to know what's going on on this side of the door, but Martha shakes her head and doesn't reply.

She doesn't want to miss a word of mine, doesn't want me to stop. Her eyes try to choose between my feet and my face and Lenny too now and then. He can't dance like I can because of his leg that's too short, but he does move his upper body and clap his hands. She would have liked to look everywhere at once, there's so much to see.

"Za zoo za zoo," I sing while swinging my arms.

Martha's mother comes to have a look as well, with just her head at first, which turns red when she sees Lenny and me.

She always glows when we're around. We don't know why. She'll touch Lenny's white hair and ask if it's real, or she'll caress my cheek, and if I'm wearing new pants, she'll pinch them and say that the newness hasn't been pinched out of them yet.

Occasionally she'll ask about my mother, but I don't like that. My sister, Anneka, won't let me tell the truth. I'm supposed to say that our mother is even better than yesterday, always better than yesterday, even though the more time goes by the less light she can bear, even though she stays in bed and at the slightest sound in the house asks for Mone.

Martha's mother beams. She pushes the door open with her hip. That Bing, I can see her thinking. My, just look at me, she is also thinking, although when the refrain comes around, she has already forgotten who she is. She dances along. She moves her hands back and forth as if she were wiping the windows.

"Za zoo," she sings.

"Za zoo za zoo zay," I sing.

I get lots of applause. Not just from Martha and

her mother, but also from Lenny, whose lungs are wheezing even though he hasn't done anything that could make him short of breath, and from a neighbor lady farther down.

Martha rolls her eyes and embraces her own throat. "That's the most beautiful hello I ever got in my life up till now," she says.

"Thank you," I say.

"Hello. Hello?" says Martha's mother. "Was that a hello? From whom?"

Martha swoons.

"Who would a hello be from?" she says, and she fills her large lungs with air. She is going to name a name—his name. She has already practiced it a lot: Dani Bennoni. At night she whispers it to herself a thousand times a thousand times—Dani Bennoni— until she falls asleep. I know that from my sister, Anneka, and she knows it from Martha herself.

"Dani Bennoni!" she says.

Lenny and I look at each other and then down at the toes of our shoes. *We* didn't mention that name. *We* didn't say that name out loud. We can't claim the name isn't serving us well, though.

"Dani Bennoni?" sings Martha's mother. She

hooks her arm into Martha's and gives it a shake. Her eyebrows go up and down and she purses her lips. She doesn't know whether she should be glad and whether she should stoke the fire; boys aren't heaters.

Lenny and I smooth our faces.

"Bennoni the soccer player," I say. With that I have not said too much.

Martha's mother smiles.

"The soccer player," she says, and she nods. She is thinking of a foot and a ball and a goal, and she is glad that it makes her see something.

"Yes, yes," she says.

"Yes," I say in a measured tone. I clamp my mouth shut, and I hope they notice that my shoulders are suddenly drooping.

Martha sees only what's in her own head. She slaps her hand to her temple and shakes it, as if her temple were hot and she just burned herself.

"Oh," she says. "To think I almost forgot." She gives me a nudge. "Say hello back, Bing. Say hello to Dani."

"But you don't have to sing," says Martha's mother. "Just say hello."

"I'll do that," I say. "Someday," and I bow my head. I drag my feet off the front step.

Martha and her mother fall silent and frown.

Martha makes a sound in the shape of a question mark.

Her mother calls on a saint and looks from me to Lenny, who stands beside me as if he were hung on a nail.

I make sure I play it as well as Lenny. I pluck at Mone's shorts and look at his shoes on my feet. My spirits have fizzled; even a blind person could see that.

"Why, of course!" Martha's mother says all of a sudden, and she gropes around in her apron pocket.

Her hand appears under my face. It smells like caramel. She turns it over, opens it. There are strings and buttons in it, but also pieces of toffee.

"We're waiting for a reward, of course," she says. She twists the paper wrapper off one of the toffees and pops it into her mouth. The other two are for me and Lenny.

"No, no," I say, and I look away.

Martha leans over, and her face hovers next to her mother's hand.

"No, no?" she asks. "Bing says no no to a treat?"

"Uh," I manage, and I shrug my shoulders. On

another day I would say yes yes and smile, that's for sure, but with a toffee in my mouth I can't keep looking sour.

Martha straightens and asks Lenny over my head whether he knows what's wrong with me.

Lenny plays it better all the time.

"Tss," he breathes, and he shrugs his shoulders just like I did and wheezes from his lungs as if there were holes in them. "It's just that maybe we can't say hello back. We're not sure if we'll be seeing Dani again."

Martha looks startled and pats her cheek a few times, so as not to turn pale.

"What do you mean?" she asks. "Did he get some news?"

Lenny hesitates for a moment and looks at me.

I raise my shoulders almost imperceptibly.

Lenny has a practiced eye.

"No," he says. "No."

"Dani doesn't want to see me anymore, that's what," I say quickly.

"Yeah," says Lenny. "Bing wants to learn how to play soccer from him, but he says that he doesn't want to teach Bing. That it's impossible. That he has the wrong legs. The wrong arms."

Martha and her mother look at my legs, at my arms.

"Dani says," says Lenny, "Dani says that you have soccer players and—" He sighs and rubs his middle finger over his thumb. He takes his time. The word that Dani too was just looking for he tries to find in his head and say, but it's gone. It's gone no matter how he organizes his thoughts.

"Uh . . . other kids," he says in the end.

We wait for an answer from Martha and her mother.

Their tongues will be sharp, their breath scorching. If there's any hair on your face, it will be removed. Martha and her mother are women. They have to stand up for children. At the very least, they'll have to start hissing and spitting from anger as if they had eaten a spoonful of mustard, and curse, and say that Dani Bennoni has no manners, is a bully. What kind of man will he amount to? If I don't learn how to play soccer from him today, Dani can forget about Martha, because you don't start a future with a young man who doesn't want to do anything for a kid, for a poor kid like me.

In our heads, Lenny and I already see Martha and Martha's mother striding down the street in the direction of Dani's house. They are going to let him have an earful.

In reality, they don't budge.

Martha's mother chews on her Lutti.

Martha scratches behind her ear and pulls a strand of her auburn hair forward and sticks it in her mouth.

They both take another look at my legs and my arms and at Mone's soccer clothes.

"Hm," they sigh at the same time, and they carefully move their heads as if there were porcelain plates on them. "Other kids, other kids."

"We all have our talents," says Martha's mother.

"You do sing well, Bing, and you dance like they do in the movies," says Martha. "And aren't you good with your hands? How's your paper-and-cardboard house coming along? That's what you were making, wasn't it?"

I raise my hands.

"Good, really good," I say.

"So?" says Martha.

"But he wants to *play soccer*," says Lenny.

"Oh," says Martha's mother.

"That's right," says Lenny, and he stamps on the ground.

THREE

To Dani Bennoni's feet I say that I think Martha acted funny. I wait for Dani to react, but his feet continue to lie where they are, and so do his father's feet. They have put their Ford up on wooden blocks and are both lying under it. It looks like they were run over.

Not much more than cursing has been done here. The door to the house is open. An upstairs casement window bangs. The morning mail lies unopened where it always lies, on the privet hedge. All attention is on the Ford.

Lenny nudges me. He points at the ground with his chin and widens his eyes.

"Say it again," he whispers. "Say it again, he didn't hear you. Martha acted funny. Tell him."

I bend over as far as I can. I can't see Dani's face. I can't see farther than his knees.

"Dani," I say. "Dani?"

His legs move. He heard me. From under the truck comes a groan. "What is it this time?"

I hand the ball under my arm to Lenny and get down on my hands and knees, with my head near the ground and near Dani's feet.

"Nothing, Dani," I say.

"Then go fish," says Dani. "That's a waste of time too."

If I want him to see me, I first have to know where in the dark his face is. His voice leaves no doubt: his head is here and will stay here, *under* the truck, and we better make sure we get away. Under the Ford, work is being done.

"The hammer," says Dani's father.

The tools are on Dani's side. Something rattles over there. He says, "Here, Dad, be careful."

Dani's father is careful. He starts hammering over on his side. The truck clangs. I have to plug my ears, as shrill as the racket is.

When it's quiet again, Dani's feet and his father's feet are shaking with laughter.

"What what?" asks Dani.

"What what what?" asks his father.

It takes a couple of seconds before it dawns on me

that they're laughing about the joke they made—first they didn't hear anything because of the hammering and later they were deaf, what what what. I act as if I didn't get it.

I say, "Nothing. I only said that we saw Martha and that we were supposed to say hello from her and that we think she acted funny—Martha, that is." I look up at Lenny to see whether I should top that off with something. "Lenny thought so too," I say.

Lenny gives me a nudge. I almost lose my balance.

"Honestly," I say. "We told her we'd seen you, and you should have seen her face." With my eyes I tell Lenny that I'm playing a dangerous game, but that I'm not lying. When Martha got Dani's hello, her face did change, in front of our very eyes—that's the truth and nothing but the truth.

Lenny considers for a moment, then grins. That's true, he means.

I grin back.

We both look at Dani's feet. We wait until the feet turn into whole legs.

Here they come.

The low dolly Dani is lying on rolls out from under the Ford.

"What what what?" he asks.

Lenny and I look down at him for a few seconds.

"That her face changed," I say.

"And she acted funny?" asks Dani. He raises himself up on his elbows. "So what did she do?"

I look at Lenny and Lenny looks at me to see what our reply will be. We shrug our shoulders at the same time. It's a good thing we both pull down the corners of our mouths so that our faces change. It seems like we're imitating Martha, even though we don't mean it that way. Now that we can see it on each other, we suddenly don't know our limits anymore. Incredible what a funny face Martha made.

"Oh?" says Dani, and he hums a little bit. He wants to sit up straight. The question of why Martha looked that way and shrugged her shoulders is burning on his lips, but he doesn't get the chance to ask it out loud. His father's foot comes at him from the side. It kicks the dolly.

"Dani, the wrench," he calls out from under the Ford. "The crescent wrench."

Dani quickly lies down as if his father had thrown him on the ground with his voice. He hits his head, forgets to moan. In his haste, he still manages to grab the wrench before he rolls under the truck on his dolly.

Dani's father hisses with impatience. He curses Dani and a nut that's too much and a bolt that doesn't want to come loose. He curses in a foreign language.

Right near my ear Lenny says, "Kick it in. Now."

I frown.

Lenny points from the ball to Dani Bennoni's feet. "In a manner of speaking," he says. "Kick it in."

I swallow once.

"Go," I say. Lenny always says that too if he doesn't want to put up with any bull. I squat down. "Dani?"

Dani's body stiffens.

I clear my throat.

"I don't think Martha acted funny because you don't want to teach me how to play soccer," I say. "I don't think so. I said hardly anything about that. I also didn't tell her that you're in hock to me and that you don't have any money left."

I press my lips together and smile, in case Dani not only hears me but sees me as well. Not a word I said is a lie. If you say what you think somebody else thinks, you're not lying. You only thought wrong. Now Dani just has to think a little to our advantage, then things will go according to plan. He will teach me to play soccer. He will teach me to play soccer, and my brother will be proud of me when he comes back. Look at all the things you can do, he'll say.

Lenny and I wait for Dani's dolly. It should start moving. It shouldn't take long. What Martha thinks of Dani won't be a matter of indifference to him, I imagine. One is the spark; the other is the fire. That's the way it always goes between people.

Dani's father bursts out laughing because the bolt that made him curse finally comes loose. He wriggles over the ground on his back, crawls out from under the Ford, and plucks his cap off one of the headlights. The bolt in his hand he throws in an arc across the street and into the grass on the other side, and then he proudly puts his cap on as if it were a crown. He raises his arms.

"The technique!" he cries. "The technique!"

"Bravo," Lenny and I cry. "Bravo."

We clap our hands for Dani's father. Our enthusiasm doesn't get very far because Dani startles us.

He suddenly shoots out from under the Ford and almost runs into our legs. There he is, lying at our feet with his eyes half closed and his index finger pointing in my direction.

"You better watch what you say, Kessels," he whispers loudly, and he shakes his finger. "Tell Martha she can think what she wants. I'm not going to teach you how to play soccer. That's all I have to say."

"I want to know how for Mone," I say. "Not for Martha."

Dani shuts his eyes and briefly shakes his head. He makes his lips fat.

"You heard me," he says when he looks at me again. "I'm not doing it. I'm not."

"You have to," I say. "You promised."

"I didn't promise you anything," says Dani. "You have to take things as they come."

"Well," says Dani's father, who is busy with his own thoughts. He walks around the truck and breathes a little prayer. His face expects an engine that's dead.

He climbs in behind the wheel and sits up, ready to start cursing, but when the engine first sputters and after a second starts running as if it had never broken down, he grows until his cap touches the roof.

"Yeah!" he cries above the noise. "Yeah!"

Dani nods—first because he is glad for his father and then because he agrees with himself.

"Yeah," he says. "Yeah," and he nods even more resolutely than at first. "Tell Martha I never do anything I don't want to do." He pats the side of the truck with his hand and goes over to stand beside his father. "Tell her that. And if she doesn't want to hear it, shout it."

FOUR

"Rotten germ," says Martha.

"Rotten jerk," says Lenny, wheezing, and we snicker at Martha's slip. Martha meant what she said, though.

Dani can get the worst disease there is.

She turns around and opens the front door up wide so the pungent smell of celery can go outside and we can look down the short hallway into the kitchen that is fuller than it was earlier.

Martha's mother is standing at the stove. Sitting at the table are Theresa Dombrecht, who never says anything, and Anneka, my sister.

"There," says Anneka to me. "It's little brother."

I don't answer.

Theresa and Anneka and Martha's mother look over at Martha, who is standing straddle-legged in the doorway with her back to us. She jabs her thumb over her shoulder in our direction.

"Dani Bennoni," she says, as if she were talking about the germ itself. "First I get a hello from him, with a song, and now Bing comes to tell me Dani Bennoni says I shouldn't act so funny. As far as I know, I haven't left the house, so don't ask me what he means and where he gets the idea that I'm acting funny."

We peer around her elbow and see Theresa's mouth and Martha's mother's mouth drop open. Only Anneka is not looking at Martha. Anneka is looking at me.

"Are you in the middle of this for something?" she asks with a nod in my direction.

Martha takes a step to the side so that they can all look at me. They turn their heads a little, with their ears toward me.

"The middle of what?" I ask.

Anneka slams the table with the flat of her hands and pushes back the bench she's sitting on.

"The middle of *what*, he asks. The middle of *what*," and she shows her two hands and the space in between them. "The middle of *that*!"

She reaches across the table for the jar of raisins. She takes a handful before nodding in my direction.

"If you're playing dumb, little brother, that's not

half bad, as dumb as you can look." She pops the raisins into her mouth and starts chewing with the fastest jaw in the world.

"I don't know what you're talking about," I say, and I curl my toes. I peer sideways at Martha, who is standing beside me.

She looks back.

If I start shaking right now or coughing or swallowing, she will think it's suspicious. I don't shake. I don't swallow. I only cough a little.

Lenny and I are not committing any sins. We are not claiming we truly, word of honor, are not in the middle of this for something. If we were to do that, a cross would grow on our foreheads, or maybe we'd turn black all over. We're not lying.

I say, "We only came over to tell you what Dani said."

Anneka snorts through her nose.

"What Dani said," she says. She lays her hand on her chest and looks like the saints in devotional pictures. "What Dani said. What Dani God the Father said."

Martha gurgles once.

"Could I be exaggerating?" asks Anneka. She

picks at her teeth, at a piece of raisin stuck there. "It's not because Dani Bennoni thinks something that it actually is that way."

"But," I start.

"But what?" asks Anneka, and she turns around on the bench. "Is little Kessels going to defend the big Bennoni?"

"No," I say.

"Be quiet, then. If Bennoni points his finger in your direction one day, you'll actually stop moving from that day on, I'm sure of it. You're already just as bad as Mone. Just like you, he thought it was so terribly important what Bennoni thought of him, and we know how that turned out. Our Mone, the hero, is no longer here, but Bennoni is."

"For the time being," says Martha's mother.

"Don't roll your eyes, little brother," says Anneka to me. "Sometimes I think you're Bennoni's dog. If he points his finger at you one day, you'll go and stand in a glass case from early in the morning till late at night, with your hands in the air and a sign around your neck: I was chosen by Dani God the Father when he pointed One Finger at me."

They're all snickering.

"Chosen by Dani God the Father, who wanted to go dancing with Martha Vochten once, la-de-da, but lost his chance one day because he thought Martha Vochten acted funny!"

The four of them burst out laughing—Martha's mother with her head above the steaming pot and a spoon in her hand, Theresa Dombrecht and Anneka leaning against each other.

Martha is shaking against the doorframe. "Acted funny!" she giggles.

I look down at the ground. I can feel I'm blushing.

If Dani Bennoni nods at me in church on Sunday, I sit up for him like a dog—Anneka's right. If he winks and nods at me, I become a dog you pat on the head. If Dani winks and nods and also gives me a sign to go to the Daring Club clubhouse in a little while to wait for him, I do that. I'm probably a dog.

Martha's enjoyment is the first to pass. She pokes her knee into my thigh from the side.

"Did he really say that, 'acted funny'?" she asks.

"More or less," I say.

"Oh, that Dani," says Martha's mother. "Save him the grief."

"Is he a Souby's savings point, maybe?" asks Anneka. "If we have to spare him, he has to spare us, too. We're all in pain if we keep quiet."

She gets up from the table and hesitates on one leg.

I see that she is looking at my clothes. She is taking them off, I can see it—Mone's jersey, Mone's shoes and socks, Mone's shorts. In my mind I'm standing there on the front step with almost no clothes on.

I cringe as if I were a snail and she were gripping a jar of salt. My blood throbs in my toes.

"Go on back to that Daring clubhouse," says Anneka, "or wherever Dani God the Father appeared to you."

She looks around at Theresa and the rest of the kitchen, then slowly walks toward me. "Go back to Our Lord Dani and tell him that he's a few sizes too big for his britches. Tell him that Martha can make sure that no girl wants him anymore, if he doesn't offer an apology today, let's say *before* lunchtime. To Martha. 'I offer you my apologies, Miss Martha. I, Fool Bennoni, act funny. You, Miss Martha Vochten, do not act funny.' That's his text. Tell him that. And better watch out; the soup's almost on the table over here."

Anneka smiles.

I look to see whether Martha agrees with that smile.

She does. She's even grown an inch taller. Anneka just voiced what all the girls are thinking.

"Off you go," Anneka says to us.

"You're not the boss around here," I say, but—tsk, tsk, she has no patience. She shoves Lenny and me both off the doorstep and says that there's nothing for me to do but obey, and if I don't, the girls can make sure in no time that things will end badly for us as well.

"Take off those clothes," she hisses at the back of my ear. "Everybody can see that those are Mone's clothes. They look ridiculous."

"I'm going to learn how to play soccer," I say.

"You, play soccer? Tell me another one," says Anneka.

"Mone will think it's great that I know how to play soccer," I say. "Me, playing soccer."

Anneka shuts her mouth. She takes a step outside, pulls the door against her back, and waits for a moment.

"If he comes back," she says. She touches the

hairpin in her hair. "I already told you: *if* he comes back. Please don't start every sentence with 'Mone.' We already have our mother for that."

Inside, Martha and Martha's mother and Theresa burst out laughing again. I don't know what the joke is, but I believe it's me.

"Him? Never!" somebody inside says. "Not even if God teaches him, God the Father Himself."

Anneka closes her eyes. Sometimes she's ashamed of me, I think. She pulls the tips of her collar together with her thumb and forefinger and lets her other hand rest on her chest, to hold her heart.

"Are you still there?" she asks, without looking to see if I've already gone.

"No," I say as I walk away. "I'm going to find a hole in the ground, and then I'm going to crawl into it."

"Do that, we'll miss you," I can hear her say before she disappears inside and slams the door.

FIVE

It takes a while before Lenny has caught up with me. I slow down for him, almost come to a standstill, but at the same time I ward him off from a distance with my hand, and hold a finger to my lips. I don't want him to say anything. I want to say something myself, and I'm not going to shout. Not until he's standing in front of me and has regained his balance am I going to say it.

I say, "Honestly." I look at him squarely, plant my feet next to each other, and straighten my back.

"What honestly?" asks Lenny, and he tucks the ball under his arm.

"What's not right about me?" I ask.

Lenny is surprised and raises his eyebrows. He sizes me up from top to toe and makes a puffing sound.

"Everything is right about you," he says.

"Yeah," I say, and with my head I indicate Martha's

house, where they just finished laughing at me. "And now honestly."

Lenny grabs my shoulder and squeezes it. "Honestly," he says. "I can't think of anything that I don't think is right."

He swears it. He spits between his fingers.

I push a little air out of my lungs to let Lenny hear that I only half believe him.

"What, hmph?" says Lenny. "You're making an entire house out of paper and cardboard, not me. I can't draw, you can. You can sing, I can't. I can't dance, you can. Bennoni never asked me to sit and look at him for money while he—"

My hand flashes out before I realize it, slap, on Lenny's mouth.

Lenny stares at me with huge eyes and raises his hand to his head as if wanting to make sure it's still there.

"Watch your mouth," I say.

Lenny moans once and shrinks back.

"But it's true," he hisses. "It is true."

"Is not," I say. "I may be able to dance, but just because I can do that still doesn't mean my feet are as light as Dani's. They don't jump by themselves.

They're not fast. They don't shoot off in all directions the way his do. Dani has two rats dangling from his legs. Dani's a soccer player."

"Yes," says Lenny, and he tucks the ball under his other arm. "Dani is a soccer player."

"I'll learn anyway. From him."

"Right," says Lenny. "Even if you drop dead, I know you will." He pays attention to how he plants his short leg and points over my shoulder with his chin.

"There he is," he says.

Behind me a truck drives up, honking, but it sounds like coughing. It's the Ford. Dani's behind the wheel.

My face suddenly flushes.

Dani lowers the window on the driver's side. He shows us with his hand which direction we're supposed to go, this way or that.

"Hurry up," he shouts. He jabs at us with the bumper. Go away, sit up, lie down. "Move over!" He sticks his head out the window and tugs at his eyelid with his forefinger. He nods in the direction of the truck bed.

There are bales of straw in it.

Lenny and I take a step to the side and look at the

road behind the truck. From the bed of the pickup to probably in front of their door, there is a trail of dust and fallen wisps.

"Left a bit of a mess," says Lenny.

"Is it getting to your lungs?" asks Dani.

"No," says Lenny. "I'm making an observation. A whole barnful's blown off."

Dani chuckles once. He closes his eyes. At first I think he's still laughing about what Lenny said, but then I see that he's doing a stunt, that he can drive with his eyes shut even though he's really not allowed to drive, not even with his eyes open. When he's almost past us, he puts his foot on the brake. He smirks at his father, who's sitting next to him, then turns his face toward us.

"So, Bing?" says Dani. He moves his head in the direction of the road behind us. "Looking for something else to do?"

"No," I say. "I still want the same thing." I shake my left foot once, then my right foot. I'm thinking: if I were Dani, I'd be friendlier to me.

Dani is blind to my feet. "Otherwise you could find a dustpan and a brush," he says.

"The wind will sweep it up," I say.

"There isn't any wind," says Dani.

"Then the rain will wash it away," says Lenny. "We've been walking back and forth the whole time already. If we didn't know any better, we'd think we had learned how to play soccer."

Dani exposes his handsome teeth in a wide grin. "And who's going to win?" he asks.

"At this point, Martha Vochten," says Lenny, and he hands me the ball and nudges me in the back so that I stick my chest out.

"She says she can make sure nobody wants you anymore," I say, "if you don't offer an apology before lunchtime. And we're supposed to warn you, the soup is already almost on the table over there."

"They call you . . . uh," says Lenny, and we both act like we're looking for the word "germ."

Dani looks from me to Lenny and back.

"Well?" he asks.

"Uh . . . a germ," says Lenny.

"And you don't want to know the rest," I say.

Dani hisses once between his teeth but then decides to laugh. He raises the window a little and shakes his head. Behind the glass he raises his voice because he thinks we won't hear him otherwise. He says that Martha can call him whatever she wants.

"If she curses, I won't even curse back," he says loudly, and with his head he indicates the world that lies behind and under the Ford. "Ask her if she's got a dustpan and brush. There's work to be done. Women's work."

With his thumb and forefinger he mimics a starting pistol. His hand is the gun, and with his mouth he imitates the sound. He throws his head back and roars with laughter, together with his father. *Ha ha, go,* and off they drive in the Ford.

Lenny and I turn away from the road, our backs to the cloud of dust and the whirling wisps. We scrunch our eyes to slits and watch the way the truck heels to the left and takes the turn, up the road to Tahon's barn, where a camping place is being prepared for an army company to spend the night before moving on tomorrow.

We stand there coughing for a good long while.

"Work," I say to Lenny, and I pluck wisps out of my mouth.

"Women's work," says Lenny. He clears his throat and points over his shoulder to Martha Vochten's house.

There is movement on the front step. Theresa Dombrecht and Anneka are saying good-bye to Martha. They have their coats on. They are not going to sweep. I believe Dani didn't mean them either.

Lenny frowns because he hears me sigh. "What's the matter?" he asks.

"What do you think is the matter?" I ask. "He wants to see me sweep."

"He wants to see the women sweep," says Lenny. He closes his mouth and reflects for a moment. "Or did we get that wrong?"

SIX

The girls gape, and Martha's mother too. Martha is the only one to make a little sound when she does it, because she already knew Dani had a big mouth, but that it's a barn door, she never saw that, and it shocks her.

"Honest," says Lenny. He nods, and he knows I'm looking at him and nodding along with him because I'm supporting him. "The whole street," Lenny repeats. "Sweep up all the bits of straw, he said, the whole barnful out there on the street. It's work for women."

"And his apology?" asks Martha.

"Apology?" I ask. "I don't think he's in the mood for apologies right now. You can curse at him, he won't curse back. You can call him whatever you want."

"Is that so?" asks Martha. She makes her lips thin.

"Why should we lie?" asks Lenny.

"That's true," says Martha's mother. She looks from Lenny to me and back. She shuts her eyes tightly once and purses her lips, such good boys we are. She wants to check her apron pockets to see whether she still has a Lutti for us.

Anneka distracts her. She shakes her head, and she also shakes her forefinger in front of Martha's mother's face. It's curtains for Bennoni.

"Who were we supposed to spare?" she asks.

"Oh, that boy, how old is he?" asks Martha's mother.

"How old is he?" Anneka sneers. "Old enough to know better."

"I'm not so sure," says Martha. She sticks out her hand as if she were stroking a toddler's head.

"Martha," says Martha's mother. "You're shaking with spite."

"Just call it rage," says Martha, and she turns around and goes inside.

"What are you going to do?" asks Martha's mother. "Martha, what are you going to do?"

"What do you think I'm going to do?" asks Martha over her shoulder. She opens the closet and kicks off her house shoes. Between her lips she makes the sound of the wind. "Dani is not God the Father," she says. "If he wants to be the boss, he'll have to find another gal."

She grabs her coat, works her feet into her nice shoes, and even takes the time to stir the soup in the pot. "I'm going to wipe up the street with Dani Bennoni," she says, and she smacks the lid on the pot. "And maybe mop it, too. And when I'm done with that, I'm going to make him unhappy."

"I'll help," says Anneka, and she stands next to Martha.

Theresa doesn't hesitate. She closes up ranks.

"You sure you want to do that?" asks Martha's mother, but she doesn't get the chance to make her sentence any longer. She has to step aside for the girls, who reach for one another's elbows and walk up the street together.

They follow the straw trail. It's a little road on the road.

Lenny and I dart after them.

"Wait!" we shout.

Lenny grits his teeth. Running is hard for him. He needs his whole body to do it. If I support his short side now and then, he forgets his legs, and takes courage again; that helps.

We catch up with Martha and Anneka and Theresa together, and start walking in front of their feet. We stick out our hands as if we're pushing a little wall toward them.

Anneka swats me and Lenny on the head, the way she swats at the goats. She's scared of the goats. Us she swats harder.

Martha curses between her teeth at us, at Dani, at everything she sees in her mind.

Theresa growls too.

From a distance, Martha's mother throws oil on the fire. "Be careful!" she calls out. "Be careful with him!" She might just as well give the girls a knife.

"Yeah, right, be careful with him," hiss Martha and Anneka and Theresa, and they look for other words for "fool" and "bully." They take off their coats and roll up the sleeves of their blouses.

"Boss Bennoni," says Martha. "Boss Bennoni." As she's walking, she looks at her hands, balls up her fists, and stretches the muscles around her mouth. She will be very careful with him.

SEVEN

Dani lets the bale of straw he's holding slip to the ground. It's a while before he straightens up. He looks at his father, raises his eyebrows, and blows air out between his lips from the heat.

"Martha and her friends," he says, and he places his foot on the bale.

"Dani and his father," says Martha. She pulls up the corners of her mouth. Her upper lip sticks to her teeth. She looks to her right, where Lenny is standing. She looks to her left, where I'm standing, and nods over her shoulder at Anneka and Theresa. She divides the spit in her mouth and lays the words she is going to pronounce ready on her tongue.

"Is anything wrong?" asks Dani. He points at Lenny and me, because we're standing there panting so hard, and looks at the coats that the girls have draped over their arms.

Martha closes her eyes and opens her mouth. She starts with a word, but has second thoughts. She thinks she'd better choose another word. Two occur to her that I have never heard come out of her mouth. She says, "Well now."

"Well now?" asks Dani.

"Yes," says Martha. "I'm wondering what I should call you in the future." She draws the corners of her mouth toward the scallops of her ears.

It's a grin she has borrowed from Anneka. I recognize it. That's the way Anneka grins when she believes she's already won before she's won.

"Is it going to remain Dani?" asks Martha. "Or is it going to be something else?"

Dani suppresses a smirk. He plucks the checkered shirt off his chest. The fabric sticks to the sweat on his skin.

"It's going to remain Dani, obviously," he says.

Lenny and I, we're holding our breath. We exchange glances and raise our eyebrows.

Lenny nods at the ball, wanting to know if he should hold on to it.

I shake my head and lay the ball at my feet. I'm going to learn to play soccer. Today before the day is out

I'm going to stand on the field with Dani and discuss our tactics.

"Obviously?" asks Martha. "It's not so obvious."

Dani chuckles. He shrugs his shoulders and shows her his hands, as if Martha is supposed to place something in them.

"Oh no?" he asks.

"Oh no," she says. "It's not as logical as all that. Everything here is yours—your father, the straw, Lenny, Mone, Theresa, Anneka, myself, Tahon's barn. The whole field out back is probably yours too, and the brickyard, and when the train comes in a little while with the men, they and their uniforms and the train will probably be yours too. As of today you evidently have the say-so. It wouldn't surprise me if you'd discovered pepper and invented the wheel. That's why I just thought I'd ask. I'm asking what I'm supposed to call you in the future."

Dani's face tightens. He blinks his left eye. He looks to his father for help, but his father raises his hands, muttering, and moves a ways off. Dani's father finds support in his tobacco and his rolling papers.

Martha turns to Anneka and Theresa. She taps her finger against her temple. "We're allowed to keep saying Dani," she decides. "Remember that."

"Just Dani?" asks Anneka.

"Just Dani," says Martha.

They all repeat it a few times, as if Dani were a new name they have to try out in different ways.

The muscles in Dani's face grow taut. He puffs out his cheeks, purses his lips, makes deep wrinkles in his forehead. He looks out from under his eyebrows in the direction of the barn to see whether his father has any ideas about what to do with the girls, but nothing more than some muttering comes out from behind his father's teeth.

Dani, just like his father, would prefer to light a cigarette and blow a cloud of smoke around himself. Just because you play on a team doesn't mean you're always able to put up with lots of people, Dani told me once.

"Where are you going, Pa?" Dani calls out when he sees his father separating himself from the wall and walking toward the front gate.

"To find out if there's anything else we're supposed to know about, and I'm thirsty," says Dani's father without looking back. "Unload the bales. Chase those flies away."

He mutters something else after that, but we don't

hear it because he's already too far away from us and Martha is talking at the same time.

"Listen," she says. "Listen."

Lenny and I listen to Dani's father's heavy boots on the road behind us, but that's not the sound Martha means.

She snaps her fingers and looks at us as if we're her class.

"Is there really no better name for him?" she asks. "A name that fits him?" She inspects Dani from head to toe as if he were going to wear the name like a coat. "It would be hard for us to call him Dani God the Father. That would almost be cursing. There's only one God who's boss."

Anneka and Theresa check their laughter just in time.

"Dani God the Second isn't good either," says Martha. She lets her thoughts browse for a few seconds. "If you have to listen two separate times, you know it doesn't seem right, doesn't make sense."

"Be normal: Dani Bennoni," Dani says suddenly. He turns his face toward her and raises his hands. "Dani Bennoni," he says. "Then that problem's solved. Neither of us will waste any time. You on me, me on you."

He points at the bale at his feet. He points at the barn. "We're supposed to turn a barn into sleeping quarters before tonight, and I haven't seen any help turn up." He grins with one corner of his mouth—he can do that well—and after that makes a gesture that clashes with it. "If you'd like to leave now with the women's association, Martha Vochten, I can keep working," he says. "Go eat your soup. It's noon. Excuse me."

Martha looks at Dani and leans back. She gapes in amazement. She looks at Dani's shoulders, at his forehead, his hips. She shakes her head and lays her hand on her chest to feel whether she's still alive. She nods. She nods harder and finally says, "To think I didn't see that before."

A grin slides across her face, a real one. She turns her palms up and weighs the silence on her hand. She sticks her middle finger and thumb up at the same time, as if she were holding a card with a name on it, which she reads a few times in silence. Finally she also says it aloud.

"Dani Mussolini."

Air gets stuck in Theresa's and Anneka's throats.

The saliva that Martha collected she spits on the ground in front of her own feet.

Dani Mussolini.

Anneka taps her upper lip. "Perfect," she says. "Just his size. Fits him like a glove."

The girls look at one another in turn and hesitate for a moment, and then the three of them make like they're bursting out laughing. It's the laughter of crows. They're making noise more than anything else. They throw their arms around one another's waists, as if they can't stand up all by themselves, and walk through the gate and down the road.

EIGHT

The shaking of Lenny's head is almost invisible to the naked eye. If it were possible, he would move only the tip of his nose. He looks out the corner of his eye at me, wets his lips, and takes a deep breath. It is a sigh that he heaves, but then in reverse.

"I wouldn't take that," he says, like he's talking to himself.

Carefully I look up, at Dani.

Dani hears nothing of what is happening under his nose. He follows the girls with his eyes. His arms hang down beside his body. Between his lips there's a wisp of straw. His face is deadpan. When the girls' voices hit the higher registers, his left eye twitches.

"Well, they're having fun," I say in his stead.

I should know it's better to say nothing in Dani's stead.

His gaze releases itself from the road, slides down, and hovers at the height of my face.

"Hadn't you better keep your mouth shut?" he says.

He nibbles on the straw, bites off a piece that he spits out, and puts the rest in his mouth again as if it were a thought he hasn't completed.

I can see the darkness in his head. If you're his father, you can disagree with him. A dog like myself, he'll rip its throat open.

"Did I ask for your opinion?" he inquires.

I recoil.

Lenny takes a step back, just like I do.

Dani leans over and shakes a finger in front of my nose.

"Stay put," he says, and he grabs me by the chin, turning his thumb and forefinger into a vise. He pulls me toward him.

I have to imitate a fish, one that's struggling on dry land.

"Dani," I try to say.

"Yes?" he responds, and he sucks in his cheeks and mimics me. He holds my face in front of his, and his forehead brushes mine. His breath smells sweet and sour, like the milk and the cow at the same time. He stands with his entire body over me. I think he's even standing beside and behind me.

I cringe.

It's the first time I have it: a faint heart. Never before have I been afraid of him. Not once in all those times we were alone together.

With his smart forehead he can butt me, with his handsome teeth he can bite, with his quick eyes he can drill me into the ground. In the Daring Club clubhouse, Dani is just as tall as here, but here he towers over me.

"Dani," I say. "Let me go."

Dani chuckles once out of the corner of his mouth.

"Let me go?" he says. "You mean: Let *me* go." He grabs his chest with one hand, as if he had to hold himself together, but meanwhile plants his other hand on top of my head and pulls me down by my hair.

I have to follow his hand, unless I want to see clumps of hair on the ground soon or want to look behind myself forever. My eyes fill with tears.

Dani shoves the side of my face into the straw.

Lenny doesn't know what to do. Where should

he start? Compared to Dani he's a moth. He flutters around us, almost trips on my lower legs.

"Don't! Dani, don't!"

"Don't. Lenny, don't," says Dani, as if Lenny had been mistaken about the name. He just plain hauls out with his foot.

Lenny gets a shoe in his chest and falls over backward into the hedge. Branches snap, but they could just as easily have been Lenny's bones—the kid is made of lame brushwood.

"Lenny?"

I want to turn, but Dani has me in the vise. I grope behind my back with one hand. I grasp at the empty air beside me. I look for Dani above my head, until I get hold of a piece of cloth. It's a sleeve. I yank on it as if it were Dani's skin. I hear his shirt tear at the seams.

Dani panics. His hands can't overpower me. He gets his leg into the act. He lets his knee come down on my upper arm like a rock.

I yelp in pain. I squirm in rage, kick wildly first with one leg and then the other. The only things I make contact with, though, are the bale and myself. I kick open my blisters. The pain cuts like knives through my toes.

In a single slice, my tendons have been severed. I can hardly stand.

My mouth is buried in the straw. I inhale dust. I struggle under Dani's hand. The dust wants to get out of my lungs. I need air, but there's no air anywhere. I need new lungs, but first these have to go. I cough and I cough. There is no way I can stop.

"Yeah, kid?" says Dani right above my head.

He's drooling, I think. He's drooling in my neck. He tugs at my hair as if he wants to make a ponytail of it at all costs. Soon my ears will be positioned next to each other. Soon I'll hear with the back of my head.

I wonder if this is the best moment. Shall I kick Mone's shoes off now? Shall I tell Dani what I know and what he still doesn't know? After that, shall I say, "What's wrong? Suddenly I'm not hearing you anymore"?

Dani raises me up a ways.

"Have you learned your lesson?" he hisses, his mouth right in front of my face so I can feel the moisture of his breath. "Will you be able to play soccer now? Will it work, do you think? See how I punish people?"

He jerks my head back—there's nothing to it, I'm a doll—but it's the last thing he can do to me.

I catch a glimpse of Lenny, who's standing like an acrobat on top of the straw bale. He's balancing on his good leg and holding a shoe over his head. He hauls out, slugs Dani on the ear with it—ow—with that block heel that's so much bigger and harder than a normal heel, and jerks me back by my collar.

Dani Bennoni mows the air with his arms. He takes a step forward, a step to the side. He teeters like a drunk and finally slams his head against the door of the Ford.

Ow, I think again, but I don't wait to find out how badly Dani fell.

"Come on," Lenny and I say to each other at the same time, and we pump air through our clenched jaws, and we sprout wings. We don't touch the road, we skim over it. I help Lenny fly.

NINE

Martha's mother calls on all the saints she knows, especially the saints who stand up for children and the less fortunate. She walks toward us with her arms spread wide, and just about picks us both up at the same time.

"Crumpled boys!" she cries. She gives Martha a sign to go hang on the handle of the pump.

We have to be washed and ironed.

She draws me to her and without further ado holds my head under the gushing water. After that she pulls Lenny over and holds him over the pump basin. She rubs her bare hand over our faces. She doesn't care that we're spluttering from the cold. We're allowed to struggle in protest and make her floor and her apron and if necessary her entire kitchen wet. It's for our own good, she says.

She throws a towel over our heads as if we were

hares that you catch with a coat, and wedges us under her armpit to keep us under control.

I squeal like a pig.

Lenny squeals even louder; he is easily bruised.

Martha's mother has no ears for it. She says, "Now, now," and helps Lenny tie the laces of his shoes, and pushes us into chairs side by side next to the stove.

We are two new children of hers, that's how she looks at us. She takes a few steps back to see if we've already grown. With her hands on her hips, she waits until we're breathing normally again.

My heart goes crazy. It's beating even harder than before, I think.

There are different sides to my body. My legs quiver as if the running had scared my muscles. My hands are cold down to the bone. I rub myself warm, but it doesn't help. Every part of me stays cold, although sweat meanwhile breaks out on my back. What's more, inside it's as if I've just been slipped out of the oven.

In my head there is room for thoughts I'd rather not have. I see Dani again and the straw. I see a head slam into a truck door and make a sudden movement with my hands, the way you sometimes do when you've almost fallen asleep.

It flashes through my mind that Dani has never hurt me before. Never. As soon as I think that, my eyes fill with tears.

Martha's mother opens her arms.

"Now then," she says. "Now then." She rubs her hands together and watches expectantly for a story to come out of our mouths.

Lenny and I immediately look down at our laps. We have hands that itch and don't want to lie still.

One of Lenny's forefingers moves back and forth.

I have to watch my mouth, says the finger.

From the corner of my eye, I see Martha and Theresa and Anneka shuffle closer. Sand crunches under their shoes. They think they're moving as calmly as angels, but they forget that their breathing is uneven, their sweat still fresh. They themselves haven't completely gotten over their encounter with Dani Bennoni. The rims of Martha's eyes look red.

"Now then," says Martha's mother again, and she leans toward us.

"It's Dani," whispers Lenny.

"All morning it's been Dani," says Martha's mother.

"He got angry," says Lenny.

"Angry?" asks Martha's mother.

"Yes," says Lenny. "At us."

"At me, really," I say.

"Poor thing," says Anneka.

Martha's mother makes a little sound with her tongue and with her hand she imitates Anneka's mouth: open once and then firmly shut. Maybe she'd better keep her distance and go stand behind the table.

Anneka snorts through her nose. She folds her arms in front of herself like a shield. "He shouldn't turn things around," she says. "It all started because of him."

Martha's jaw drops. She frowns at Anneka.

"Because of who did it all start?" she asks.

"Because of him," says Anneka.

"Not true," says Martha. "Because of me." Entirely superfluously she points at herself and nods as she does this. Her lower lip quivers.

Martha's mother growls.

"Stop it," she says, snarling a little. She chops the kitchen into two. One part she pushes toward Anneka, the other part is for Martha.

Anneka has to go stand against the wall behind the table, disappear into the jar of raisins if possible.

Martha has to go sit down on the chair by the door, and be quiet, most of all be quiet. She doesn't succeed. She rubs her eyes and mutters that nobody needs to lecture her. Dani over there just lectured her, and she moves her head in the direction of the Tahon property.

"Lecture Anneka for once, Mother," she says. There's too much air around her voice. "She's always on Bing's case. That poor kid."

As soon as I hear my name, I stiffen.

Anneka looks at me.

"That poor kid," she says. "Be glad you don't have a brother like him."

"His eyebrow's bleeding," says Martha. "He's bleeding."

"I can see that," says Anneka. She nods at me and looks down her nose. "What do you want me to do? Lay my finger on the cut and wait until I'm joined up with him? We all have some hurt somewhere that doesn't heal."

"It's not about you for once," says Martha. "It's about him. Bennoni lit into him—probably because we lit into Bennoni."

"It's little brother's own fault," says Anneka. "He

has to learn that he's better off hanging around with idiots his own age."

"He's looking for a big brother," says Martha. "It's written all over his forehead in great big letters!"

"He's got me, doesn't he?" Anneka exclaims.

Martha wants to shout something back, she's already smiling a mocking smile, but Martha's mother throws up her arms and sings out a line, "We deserved it, so much love, so many sorrows."

She continues to stand in the middle of the kitchen and look at the ceiling and the sky above it. Will Martha and Anneka please keep their mouths shut, she begs. As far as she's concerned, a lot of love and sorrow have already come together in the kitchen today.

"For heaven's sake."

She walks over to the cupboard and reaches for a little white box on a shelf above her head and meanwhile tells me to sit up straight because she wants to see my face. She places the little box next to herself on the stove and lays my head back in her hand.

Martha and Anneka clamp their lips shut.

Theresa has gone over to stand between them like a referee. If anybody dares to let out a peep, she'll pull out a card.

Martha's mother examines the cut that runs through my eyebrow. She sighs with concern and makes a little sound with her tongue against her teeth.

"Did he hit you?" she asks.

"No," I say.

"No no," she says. "I can see that."

"He pushed me into the straw," I say.

"Right," says Martha's mother. "And then that cut just showed up all by itself."

"Will I have a scar?" I ask.

"If I don't take good care of it, yes," she says.

"Hm," I go, and I don't dare to say out loud that Martha's mother shouldn't make the wound terribly clean. "Mone has a scar too," I whisper to her. "And Dani Bennoni has one, too, on his stomach."

Martha's mother pulls up one corner of her mouth, as a favor to me.

"And you should certainly take an example from them," she says. "What shall I sprinkle into it so it will get infected? Sugar? Should it be a scar with or without extra skin?"

"Make it one with," says Anneka on the other side of the kitchen, her mouth filled with raisins. "Where's the sugar?"

Theresa and Martha and Martha's mother gasp at the same time, but all three decide not to make any remarks and to find me more important.

Martha's mother takes a bottle and a wad of cotton wool out of the little white box. She says I'll get a Lutti if I just grit my teeth now, and she presses the wad against the mouth of the bottle and makes a twisting motion with her hands until the iodine leaks through the cotton wool and her fingers.

The kitchen suddenly smells like my mother. It's the smell that hangs in the curtains of her bedroom. She lives in bed, but she never sleeps. Three months ago she woke up for the last time, I think. That was the morning Mone left. She has continued to keep a vigil ever since, half sitting up in bed, because you never know if Mone might be coming home now—or now.

Without warning, Martha's mother presses the cold wad against the cut on my eyebrow. She rips the cut open even more, I think.

For a couple of seconds it turns black in front of my eyes. I want to push Martha's mother away, but she slaps my hand and shushes in my ear.

"Look at what a man I've got here," she shushes,

and she repeats it a few times. That dampens the fire in my head a little.

I close my eyes. I don't cry. I would like to cry, though.

"Brave boy," says Martha's mother after a while, and she blows the heat from my face. "You're a brave boy." She sings to distract me. "Za zoo," she sings. "Za zoo za zoo zay."

Next to me, Lenny chuckles.

"Dance, Bing, dance," he says.

"Hm," I go. I would most like to have a new jersey and a new pair of shorts on, and new socks and a new cap too. Then Martha's mother would see that they weren't pinched out yet. Then she'd pinch the newness out of my clothes. Then she'd just pinch me, grab me everywhere, draw me close to her a little. Probably she would kiss me on the crown of my head, but in the way only she does it. She presses her lips on my forehead and blows until that one little spot is all warm.

Martha's mother is not thinking of kisses. She keeps singing—it's not the same song anymore by a long shot—and acts as if she's dancing with me. By accident she hugs me a bit, and she presses her face into my neck. She has a warm nose.

That's okay too.

I try not to think of Dani.

When her own song is done, Martha's mother says, "There."

She places the stopper in the bottle, snaps the little box on the stove shut, and puts the bits of cotton wool into her apron pockets.

"Isn't it high time for a good talk?" she says to nobody in particular. She turns her back on everyone as if to say she really doesn't expect an answer and won't take any disagreement. She pulls the handle of the pump up and down a few times and washes her hands until they can't get any cleaner, until no more water comes out.

"Who with?" asks Martha.

"Who do you think?" replies Martha's mother, and she pivots in search of a towel for her wet hands. She finally dries them on her apron. Only when they're bone dry does she respond. "With Dani Bennoni, of course."

Lenny and I sit up.

Martha, Theresa, and Anneka straighten their backs.

Martha's mother has to laugh at us.

"I'll be careful," she says deliberately. "Very careful." She looks squarely at each of us, one by one, asking what's wrong. "I say his name and you all coil up like a spring. What makes him so special? That boy is just a soccer player. I've known a few. I know their moves—to the left if they want to go to the right, backward when it gets too dangerous."

She laughs because she herself is walking out of the kitchen backward, and she slams the door. She has the windows rattling for an unusually long time afterward. Long after she has disappeared up the street, they're still rattling.

TEN

Anneka leaves her spot behind the table and walks with measured steps over to the stove. She lifts the lid of the soup pot and sniffs at the steam that billows up to the ceiling like a celery ghost. She covers the pot again, stands still, and turns her head just a quarter turn. She waits a moment before she says anything.

Lenny and I look up at her. We push our lips forward. We knit our brows. We swallow, but Anneka doesn't see that.

"Well?" she asks.

"Well what?" asks Lenny.

"I mean," says Anneka, "what else is there to tell?"

Lenny shakes his head and shrugs his shoulders. "What should there be to tell?" he asks. "There isn't anything else to tell." His eyes dart my way for an instant.

I'm quick. I say to Lenny with my eyes that it's

okay. He's not lying. He has answered an unclear question. What else does my sister want to know?

Anneka looks around, into the kitchen, at Theresa and Martha, who have both folded their arms like they're locked. She crosses her arms as well and takes a step in Martha's direction.

"You think I don't pay little brother any mind," she says. "But you're wrong. I see everything, always."

I cough once. I'm the newborn baby Jesus. What kind of a stall is this? I'm looking out of my eyes like that.

"I don't miss a single detail," says Anneka with emphasis, and she shifts her weight to one leg. She leans back to be able to see me.

"I know, for example, that he got up very early this morning, our Bing. Did he have to wake up the roosters? Did he have to help them crow?" She chuckles at her own joke. "Cock-a-doodle-doo?"

I pop my lips and sit taller in my chair. I have nothing in particular to say. I got up with the first light of the sun. I went down the street because I had the feeling that lying in bed I was missing something, but outside it soon turned out that I wasn't missing anything. I saw the mailman on his bicycle. At Lenny's, the curtains were still shut. He didn't hear the pebbles I threw at his window. Across the street I saw a black cat lying in the grass at the side of the street. Other than that, I saw nothing out of the ordinary.

Out of the ordinary is maybe that I saw the mailman twice—and I stood for a long time staring at the cat.

I shoved the animal once with my foot to know whether it was really an entirely black one. It was a pitch-black one, and it had probably been stupid in life too. I could tell that from its head. A slightly smart animal will stay away from anything that's larger and moves. Under a train it's over with quickly for sure—if a cat ends up with its head a little wrong, a wheel will run it over before you know it. The important thing, though, is that it was a black cat and that the superstition is true. A black cat, even a stupid one, brings bad news.

"So?" asks Anneka.

"Nothing," I say.

"Nothing?" she asks. "Are you turning red over nothing?"

"I'm not turning red," I say.

"No? What kind of a color is that, then?" asks Anneka. "You're blushing." She turns around with a broad gesture toward Martha and Theresa and looks to see if they're laughing.

"He's blushing."

I would like her to be quiet.

Lenny looks at me. He moves his eyebrows up and down and lets his mouth hang open to make it clear that Anneka's mouth is going to keep blowing air.

I have been warned. She will be quiet only when I'm lying at her feet, as unmoving as the cat this morning. With a little bit of luck, no wheel will run me over.

"Well now," says Anneka, and grins—the grin I know.

I close my eyes. Anything can come out—a dead horse, a mistake I made once, which Anneka likes to call a whopper; in any case, a story that will make me smaller.

To my surprise, I hear her say she knows exactly what I did this morning, after the mailman and the pebbles and the cat.

Because nobody was up yet, I went to lie down on Mone's bed in Mone's room under the roof. I don't fit in the dent in the mattress, but if I lie on my side, I fit better. If I shut my eyes, it's as if I'm lying in Mone, and if I close my eyes tightly and run my hands over the mattress, I can feel how big he is. Then I can see before me the way Mone was when he left in May. For the rest, I don't have to change much about him. He left with an entire company on the train to we don't know where, but he probably hasn't changed much in these past three months. Lying in Mone makes me happy. When I've lain in the dent in the mattress, I'm ready to take on the day.

"I saw it through the crack of the doorway," says Anneka. "Isn't that ridiculous?"

She looks from Theresa to Martha. Because she doesn't get the result she expects, her face contorts. She had thought of applause, of a good score.

"No," says Martha after a long silence.

"No," echoes Theresa—unexpectedly. To our surprise she opens her mouth again. "What is ridiculous is that you're telling it at this particular moment," she says loud and clear. She presses her lips together as if to depict the period she places at the end of her sentence.

"You should shut up for a day for once," says Martha. "The kid would already be a whole lot happier."

"But—" says Anneka.

"Shut up," Martha interrupts her. She gets deep bowls out of the cupboard with the little glass windows. She sets the table for two and brings over the bread knife and the bread.

Lenny gets off his chair and points in the direction of the door with his nose.

"No no," says Martha when she sees him stand up. She sounds like a mother. "You two are going to eat soup first."

"I can't play soccer on a full stomach," I say.

Anneka slaps her hand over her mouth, but she can't hide the fact that she has to laugh. She looks at Theresa and at Martha, startled, and also at the door, because the door blows open.

ELEVEN

The door blows shut, that's how quickly it happens. Martha's mother doesn't lose any time. For a second I think she has different clothes on than before, red ones, but I'm mistaken. She strides in a straight line toward Lenny and me. We automatically move aside from the wind she makes.

She hangs her coat on the coat rack, takes the lid off the soup pot, and hurls it into the sink from a distance. The noise doesn't bother her a bit. Not with the ladle, no, with a bowl she snatches off the table, she dishes up soup.

Martha wants to say something, but Martha's mother gives her a look that makes her be quiet and with her eyes makes it clear that this goes for everybody. She sets the bowl down and sits at the head of the table, with a view of the kitchen. She takes hold of her spoon as if it were a garden implement and scoops up a spoonful. She scrapes the glaze on the bowl. She sucks her spoon into her mouth. This is not a moment for good manners.

Taking in food occurs along the same pathway for us as for animals. The difference is in the way the food is eaten. That's written in Anneka's *The Well-Bred Girl*, but ha ha, paper is malleable.

Martha's mother has to eat. If her hands don't have something to do right now, she'll make soup meat of everybody. She knows that.

We all know that.

We restrain ourselves.

We're almost at the point where we don't have any air left over to keep on standing. We watch expectantly for a story to come from Martha's mother's lips. We look at how much soup is left in her bowl and wonder if there isn't finally some time to tell us about how things are with Dani or what she did to him, but we practice patience. It'll come, the story.

Nothing comes.

Between the spoonfuls of soup that Martha's mother gulps down, a sound rises up out of her throat, as if the contents of her stomach were on their way up. The whole time she looks out the window. We look out the window with her, at the other side, as if the trees there might part and allow us to see the Tahon property.

Lenny shuffles over and nudges me. He curls his lips between his teeth and clamps them together. This is not the best moment to move your mouth, he means. Not.

I keep track of Martha's mother's eyes, just as he does, to see if they're suddenly darting in Lenny's or my direction, or flashing lightning. Then we'll instantly know it's not going to be a picnic for us. Dani will have had a bad fall—our fault. Her expression betrays nothing, though.

Martha can't stand it. She lays the bread knife down beside the bread with a clunk and says, "Mother, what are we waiting for? What happened?"

Martha's mother didn't hear a question mark. No question was posed. She looks around the kitchen, at Martha, at Anneka and Theresa, at Lenny and me.

"Mother," says Martha. "I'm asking you something."

For a moment it seems as if Martha's mother is going to reply, but her eyes drop down to the tabletop. She pushes back her chair and walks over to the stove.

She stands there with the soup bowl in her hand but doesn't remember what she's doing at the stove. She remembers the pot. She sees the ladle. She takes hold of the ladle but does nothing with it.

"All those young men," she says. She inadvertently glances my way, then looks at Lenny, the way she would look outside on a sunny day—as if she hadn't said anything just then and isn't thinking of anything either.

"Your ball's outside, Bing," she says. "You forgot and left it with Dani." She lets her lips curl as if she's smiling, but her eyes catch no light and her face doesn't curl with them. From the spot where she's standing, she reaches her hand out to me.

I give her my hand. Blood climbs to my cheeks.

Behind my back, Martha and Theresa and finally Anneka, too, seek each other out. They swallow half their breath. They place the tips of their fingers on their lips.

"What did you do to Dani Bennoni?" asks Martha.

"Nothing," says Martha's mother. "Nothing. When I got there, he'd already been punished."

The little hairs on the back of my neck are standing on end. I wait a moment and then ask anyway—how Dani is.

"Fine," she says. "And not fine. The mailman brought bad news this morning. He has to go. Bennoni will become a number and get a uniform. They only just found the letter. The boy is leaving tomorrow with the company that's sleeping at Tahon's tonight."

She points at Lenny and me with her chin and nods outside.

"Go play, boys," she tells us. She skims the floor with her foot like a soccer player and lifts her leg up high.

"Go play some soccer."

TWELVE

This morning, in front of Dani Bennoni's house, I see the mailman hold up a letter, and he tells me what it says.

"How do you know that, sir?" I manage to ask.

"Letters like these couldn't contain anything else," he says, and he puts the mail in its regular spot on top of the privet hedge.

The mailman goes on his way. The air in my throat stops.

I just saw the black cat. The accident is still hovering in my head.

It takes a second before I decide. Then I give the topmost letter the tap that it needs to fall next to the hedge, on account of the wind, as it were.

After that I go home, lie in Mone.

Mone has to come back, I pray. He has to be careful en route. I hear Mone whisper in my ear with his own voice that things are fine with him and that I have to have faith and have to pay attention to the things that are going on.

I keep my eyes shut and also pray for Dani Bennoni. I almost say that I'm going to miss him, but right away I cross the beginning of that sentence out of my thoughts. Why would I miss Dani?

Every time Dani winks at me and gives me the sign that I should go to the Daring Club clubhouse soon with Lenny and wait for him, I do. I'm a dog.

I have to sit down on the bench opposite the showers. I have to drop my pants onto my shoes and look at Dani Bennoni. Other than that, I don't have to do anything.

Afterward, he lifts me up on top of the bench and gives me a pat on the head with his hand. He says I'm his pal. His face is red. For the fun of it I lay my hand on his head for a change and give it a pat.

After that I pull up my pants.

Dani opens his locker and leaves its door open. He dries himself off and gets dressed. I haven't been allowed to take my eyes off him the whole time, but when it's time for him to get dressed, suddenly it's been enough; he'll pat me on the head, I'm his pal, and then the locker door has to stay open and he'll stand behind it and turn his back to me. He can't get his clothes on fast enough then—his Daring Club shorts, his jersey, his socks, his shoes. He wants to get out on the field as quickly as possible, start his training session. When he's gotten to his shoes, he always says, "Have you looked on the windowsill yet?"

The money is always lying there waiting. Lenny and I earn it by looking. I, by looking at Dani, and Lenny, by looking to see that nobody's looking, out in front of the door. I let the money drop from the windowsill into my hand. Usually I say, "It's already in my pocket," and by that time Dani's standing next to me with his shoes on. He goes to train, and Lenny and I go do something else.

Yesterday there wasn't any money, though.

While Dani ties the laces on one of his shoes, he says, "I don't have any more money."

"It's not because you don't have any more money that I won't be saving anymore," I say.

"Money doesn't make you any richer these days," says Dani.

"It's the thought of saving that counts," I say. "When Mone comes back, I want to show him how much I saved up for him."

"If he comes back," says Dani.

"You sound like my sister," I say.

"Anyway," says Dani, and he tightens his lace with a tug. "My pockets are empty."

"Anyway," I say. "You could have said that earlier."

"Think of something that's not money. Something you can also please Mone with. I'll give you that." He looks at me over his shoulder. "Is there anything you want from me?"

I blow air between my lips and drop my eyes. I'm not going to tell him that I want a lot from him and sometimes even want to be him.

"I'll have to think about it," I say.

"Do that," says Dani. "But watch your mouth in the meantime."

"Sure," I say, and as always I lock up my mouth with a key that I pluck out of the air. The key I throw away.

After that I open the outside door.

On the clubhouse doorstep, Lenny is standing guard. He always stands in the same spot, and he is always happy to see me. When there's money, I'll slip him his share as soon as I get outside. Before he makes a fist in which he lets the money jingle, he always asks if things are okay.

"Everything's okay," I'll reply, and usually I'll pretend I'm falling.

Lenny always has to laugh, as if it were the first time every time. And because he's laughing, he forgets to ask more. To avoid his asking more anyway, I make sure I keep moving. I'll say I've had enough of sitting still and that Lenny has probably had enough of standing still.

Lenny holds out his hand.

"Might as well close it," I say. "Dani has no more money. From now on he's going to pay differently."

"Oh," says Lenny.

"Yeah," I say. "I'll explain while we walk."

I look back into the changing room to see whether Dani's still looking at me, but he never is. Every time I think: I have to learn to quit looking around. After that I shut the door behind me and push it again because I never know if it's shut all the way.

When I'm done praying, I stay lying in Mone a while. Because I'm thinking of Mone and Dani at the same time, I suddenly know for sure what I have to ask Dani while he's still here. He has to teach me how to play soccer.

From the closet I take Mone's soccer clothes—his

Daring Club jersey, his shorts, his shoes. Everything's too big for me, but that doesn't matter. Dani will teach me how to play soccer.

In my room, I look for a nice white sheet of paper to make a drawing, but the nice paper is all gone. I take a piece off the roof of my paper-and-cardboard house—I still have time to finish it before Mone gets back. Then he'll get three presents from me. Money, my house, and a brother he can finally play soccer with.

The drawing is for Dani and is made up of two parts. On the left is a soccer ball, and above it, *Thank you, Mr. Dani Bennoni*, to thank him for the lesson. On the right I draw myself, and beside my mouth I write, *Long may he live*, to wish him success. The one piece I fold up and stuff into Mone's left shoe. The other piece goes into the right shoe.

After that I'm on my way to see my best friend, Lenny, who has legs of unequal length but a healthy set of brains.

At the top of the stairs a floorboard creaks under my foot. In her room, my mother is startled by it.

"Who's there?" she asks.

"It's me," I answer. "Bing."

THIRTEEN

I cross the soccer field. I grip Mone's ball under my arm. I don't feel my feet anymore. I'd love to take off Mone's shorts, they fall down so often, but I keep on walking, on through the center circle in the direction of the Daring Club clubhouse.

One time I look back at Lenny, who's gone over to the corner flag. He has sat down. That doesn't surprise me. If I let my legs decide, I'd sit down too, or no, I'd lie down here on the spot, sprawled out in the grass.

My head keeps me upright. I'm going to hang up a drawing for Dani on his locker. If there's one place he will still pass by, it's the clubhouse.

"Dani?" I call out.

His name comes out of my mouth like a fluttering bird. It doesn't even reach the clubhouse roof.

"Dani?"

Of course there's no answer.

In the brickyard, the polishing machine whines. The freight train that just thundered by the station thumps in the distance.

I cautiously close the door of the clubhouse behind me and am startled by the sudden silence. My brain is buzzing. My thoughts are bees.

Above the sinks a tap is leaking. The showers leak too. Some of the drops sing. Other drops spatter.

I go sit down on my spot on the bench, across from the showers. I lean down and untie the laces of Mone's left shoe. After that I also untie the right shoe. One by one the shoes drop to the floor.

I pull my legs up and take my feet in my hands. My socks are damp. They don't smell. They stink. They stink of Mone and me. Here and there they are brown with blood, and on my heel, the material sticks to the blister.

I won't be able to get the socks off without my skin on them, I think at first, but it almost happens by itself, almost as easily as peeling the skin off a rabbit. I have to laugh. Bare feet are wonderful.

When I put them down on the cold floor and cross it to rinse them under the shower, I groan with pleasure. "Ahh," I go, and "ooh," all by myself.

I lean against the wall and knead my feet clean. The clotted blood and the filth soak loose until the broken blisters are just pink holes in my skin. The holes itch, but even then bare feet are wonderful.

Mone's jersey has gotten wet. His shorts are soaked on one side—stupid of me.

I take everything off. Not my undershirt and my underwear at first because I don't dare, but after a while they're in my way anyhow. I throw all my clothes on a pile in front of the entry sill to the showers and find a piece of soap in a soap dish in the wall and scrub myself clean from top to bottom, the way soccer players do.

When I've had enough, I think: how am I going to dry myself off? I turn off the shower, hold my arms against my chest, and shiver once with satisfaction.

After that I get really cold.

On my spot on the bench across from the showers sits Dani Bennoni. He is sitting with his legs far apart, watching me. His mouth is no larger than a coin and his eyes are bloodshot. There's a bandage on his temple. He's biting the skin on the inside of his cheek.

I don't know how long he has been sitting there.

He hands me a dank towel. He says nothing.

To hide his uneasiness, he picks up one of Mone's shoes from the floor and examines it from all sides. He tests the shoe's elasticity between his hands, tries to fold it as if he were going to play the accordion on it. A wad of paper falls out of the toe. Dani looks at it in passing and thoughtlessly flicks the wad away with his foot.

I stop moving the towel and quickly check which shoe is still on the floor. I put on my underwear.

"Wait," I say. "Dani, wait."

The wad has turned into a frizzy lump of paper, without a beginning, without an end. It takes a while before my trembling fingers succeed in unfolding the drawing for Dani Bennoni—the portrait of myself. *Long may he live,* is written beside my mouth. It's still legible.

"Are you saying that to me?" he asks.

"Yes," I say. But I don't tell him what it all means: lots of luck, be careful, when you're coming home too.

I look at Mone's left shoe and shake my head.

"That drawing isn't important anymore," I say.

"It isn't?" says Dani.

"No," I say. I dig for the wad of paper in the shoe

and fold the drawing out as well as I can to prove it to him.

Dani sits there looking at it, defeated.

"Nice," he says.

He thinks for a moment and then crumples up the drawing he is holding in his hand.

"What are you doing?" I ask.

He stuffs the wad back in the toe of Mone's shoe and nods at Mone's ball and Mone's clothes.

"Come on," he says. "Get dressed."